Go to Sleep, Nicholas Joe

Go to Sleep, Nicholas Joe

Marjorie Weinman Sharmat

ILLUSTRATED BY

John Himmelman

Harper & Row, Publishers

Go to Sleep, Nicholas Joe
Text copyright © 1988 by Marjorie Weinman Sharmat
Illustrations copyright © 1988 by John Himmelman
Printed in the U.S.A. All rights reserved.
Typography by Trish Parcell Watts
1 2 3 4 5 6 7 8 9 10
First Edition

Library of Congress Cataloging-in-Publication Data
Sharmat, Marjorie Weinman.
   Go to sleep, Nicholas Joe.

   Summary: Tired of going to bed before everyone
else, Nicholas Joe flies from house to house all
around the world, putting children and adults to
sleep.
   [1. Bedtime—Fiction]   I. Himmelman, John, ill.
II. Title.
PZ7.S5299Gn 1988   [E]   85-45689
ISBN 0-06-025496-3
ISBN 0-06-025504-8 (lib. bdg.)

"Go to sleep, Nicholas Joe."

"I can't. The whole world's awake, Daddy."

"No, not the whole world. Plenty of children are going to bed right now. Just go to sleep, Nicholas Joe. Here's a kiss. Good night."

"Good night soon," said Nicholas Joe.

Nicholas Joe's father turned out the light and closed the bedroom door.

"Everybody else is still up," Nicholas Joe said to himself. "It's still a little light outside, and I can hear the television set downstairs, and the ice-cream truck out there, and kids playing under my window. I'm going to put the whole world to sleep."

Nicholas Joe got out of bed and pulled off his top sheet, which had purple sheep and yellow cows on it. He put the sheet on the floor and smoothed out the wrinkles.

Then he sat on the sheet. He waved his arms. "Go!" said Nicholas Joe.

The sheet and Nicholas Joe rose up and flew out the window.

Nicholas Joe flew high around the stars and the moon and showed them his new pajamas with the names of the fifty states on them.

"Now for the hard work," he said.

Nicholas Joe flew low. He flew to a small old house. A man and woman were sitting watching television.

"Time to go to bed," said Nicholas Joe. "You've seen enough television for today."

"Just five minutes more," said the man.

"No," said Nicholas Joe. "It's your bedtime."

"Oh phooey," said the woman.

Nicholas Joe led the way to the bedroom. He tucked the man and woman into bed.

"I want a glass of water," said the woman.

"Me too," said the man.

Nicholas Joe got glasses of water. "Now go to sleep," he said. He leaned over, kissed the man and the woman on the cheek, and flew out the window.

His next stop was at a big house where a woman lived with her five cats and her dog.

Nicholas Joe put out the cats for the night and brought in the barking dog. "Time for bed," he said to the woman.

"So soon?" said the woman.

"If you don't go to bed now, you won't grow up big and strong," said Nicholas Joe.

Nicholas Joe put the woman to bed.

"Wait," she said. "I need an extra blanket."

Nicholas Joe got an extra blanket.

"And I want my pillow fluffed," said the woman.

"You're stalling," said Nicholas Joe.

"I can't sleep unless my pillow is fluffed," said the woman.

Nicholas Joe fluffed the pillow. "That's it," he said. "Now you lie there and look out the window and count the stars and soon you'll be fast asleep. Pleasant dreams." Nicholas Joe flew out the window.

He flew to a farm. A farmer and his son were playing checkers in the kitchen.

"Game's over. Time for bed," said Nicholas Joe as he flew through the window.

"We have to finish our game," said the boy.

"You can finish tomorrow," said Nicholas Joe.

"I want to stay up longer," said the farmer.

"Sorry," said Nicholas Joe. "It's past your bedtime."

Nicholas Joe tucked the farmer into bed. Then he tucked
the farmer's son into bed.

"Now you're both tucked in for the night," said Nicholas
Joe.

"Yes," said the farmer, "but you have to check for
monsters in the closet."

Nicholas Joe opened the closet door and peeked inside.
"Nothing here," he said.

"Under the bed," said the farmer's son.
Nicholas Joe peered under the bed.
"Empty," he said. "Anything else?"
"I'm thinking," said the farmer.

"Think about moonbeams and all the beautiful things out
there in the night. Sleep," said Nicholas Joe as he flew out
the window.

Nicholas Joe flew to a castle. Everyone was up. The king, the queen, several princes and princesses, servants, and guards. Nicholas Joe flew around and around, locking doors and gates, closing drapes. Then he told the king and queen that it was time to go to bed.

"Not yet," said the king. "All the other kings stay up much later than this."

"Yes," said the queen. "We'll miss something exciting if we go to bed now."

"*Now*, your majesties!" Nicholas Joe commanded.

"Please may we have a glass of warm milk?" asked the queen.

Nicholas Joe made warm milk for everyone in the castle. Then he tucked them into bed.

22

"I need my teddy bear or I can't fall asleep," said one of the guards.

Nicholas Joe got a teddy bear.

"Not this one," said the guard. "The other one."

"What's wrong with this one?" asked Nicholas Joe.

"It's different," said the guard.

"Here," said Nicholas Joe. "You may have two teddy bears. But I don't want to hear another word about teddy bears. Now go to sleep!"

Nicholas Joe turned out every light in the castle. "That was a tough one," he said as he flew away.

Nicholas Joe flew
from place to place,

from house to house,

from country to country,

turning out lights,

tucking in people,

putting everyone to bed.

Then he flew back to his neighborhood. He put three children on his street to bed. "It's time," he said.

He put the neighborhood bully to bed. "I'm the boss tonight," said Nicholas Joe.

He put the ice-cream man to bed. "See you tomorrow,"
said Nicholas Joe.

At last there was only one light to be seen in the entire
world. Nicholas Joe flew toward the light. It was in his own
house.

"My mother and father are still up!"

Nicholas Joe flew back into his house. He went to his parents' room.

"Nicholas Joe," said his father, "what are you doing up?"

"I'm supposed to be up," said Nicholas Joe.

"You are?" asked his mother.

"Yes. But you're not. It's your bedtime."

Nicholas Joe tucked his parents into bed and turned off their light.

"Tell me a story," said his mother.

"Okay," said Nicholas Joe. "Once upon a time…"

"We've heard that one," said his father.

"Then dream about it," said Nicholas Joe.

Nicholas Joe kissed his mother and father. Then he went to his room and crawled into bed.

The light in his house was out. The noises of the street
were gone. It was quiet. Quiet. Like a dark warm blanket.
Nicholas Joe fell asleep.